D0065812

SCREAM STREET

Book Three

HEART OF THE MUMMY

SCREAM STREET

Book Three
HEART OF THE MUMMY

TOMMY DONBAVAND

CANDLEWICK PRESS

visit us at www.abdopublishing.com

Reinforced library bound edition published in 2012 by Spotlight, a division of the ABDO Group, PO Box 398166, Minneapolis, Minnesota 55439. Spotlight produces high-quality reinforced library bound editions for schools and libraries. Published by agreement with Candlewick Press. www.candlewick.com

Printed in the United States of America, North Mankato, Minnesota.
102011
012012

Library of Congress Cataloging-in-Publication Data

This title was previously cataloged with the following information:

Donbavand, Tommy.
Heart of the mummy / by Tommy Donbavand. —Reinforced library bound ed.
p.   cm. — (Scream Street ; 3)
Summary: Luke, Cleo, and Resus battle millions of spiders as they attempt to retrieve the heart of an ancient mummy, which is the third relic Luke needs to escape Scream Street and take his terrified parents home.
[1. Horror stories. 2. Spiders—Fiction. 3. Mummies—Fiction.
4. Werewolves—Fiction.]   I. Title. II. Series.
PZ7.D7162 He 2010
[Fic]—dc22
                    2009039355
ISBN 978-1-59961-994-1 (reinforced library edition)

For Sam, whose constant curiosity was the
inspiration for Samuel Skipstone

Meet the residents

Luke Watson

Cleo Farr

Resus Negative

Dixon

Sir Otto Sneer

Samuel Skipstone

Alston and Bella
Negative

Eefa Everwell

Doug

Dr. Skully

Niles Farr

Mr. and Mrs. Watson

Who lives where

A Sneer Hall

B Central Square

C Everwell's Emporium

D No. 2: The Crudleys

E No. 5: The Movers

F No. 11: Twinkle

G No. 13: Luke Watson

H No. 14: Resus Negative

I No. 21: Eefa Everwell

J No. 22: Cleo Farr

K No. 28: Doug, Turf, and Berry

L No. 32: Simon Howl

M No. 39: The Skullys

Previously on Scream Street . . .

Luke Watson was a perfectly ordinary boy until his tenth birthday, when he transformed into a werewolf. After it happened two more times, Luke and his family were forcibly moved by G.H.O.U.L. (Government Housing of Unusual Life-forms) to Scream Street, a community of ghosts, monsters, zombies, and more.

Luke quickly found his feet, making friends with Cleo Farr (a headstrong mummy) and Resus Negative, the son of the vampires next door. Luke soon realized, however, that Mr. and Mrs. Watson would never get over their fear of their nightmarish neighbors. With the help of an ancient book, *Skipstone's Tales of Scream Street,* he set out to find six relics, each left behind by one of the community's founding fathers. Only their combined power will enable him to open a doorway out of Scream Street and take his parents home.

With a vampire's fang and a vial of witch's blood already hidden in a golden casket beneath his bed, Luke must lead Resus and Cleo on the search for the third relic — as long as they're not scared of spiders, that is. . . .

Chapter One
The Battle

Thunder crashed as the two werewolves circled each other, fur flattened against their rippling muscles by the torrential rain. The smaller of the two creatures bared its fangs and howled, the sound echoing around the street.

The larger werewolf lunged at its opponent, ready to bite, but the small wolf was too fast to be beaten by such an obvious attack. It flung itself to the ground, back legs pulled up to protect its belly, and lashed out with razor-sharp talons, catching the aggressor's chest and drawing blood. The creature's thick fur was briefly stained red before the rain washed it clean again.

Lightning exploded over the wolves' heads, illuminating the only other figures out in the storm. A small Egyptian mummy clutched a silver-covered book while a young vampire clashed swords with an older man.

"I don't know why it took me so long to figure it out!" roared Sir Otto Sneer in delight as he swung his sword down toward the vampire's head. "If you want to beat a werewolf, *use* a werewolf!"

Resus Negative gripped his own sword and thrust it upward to block the blow. "You'll never beat Luke!"

There was a yelp as the ginger werewolf bit deep into its opponent's leg. The man smiled. "I wouldn't be so sure about that."

The smaller wolf retreated across the street. The mummy dashed over and knelt by its side. "Are you OK?" she asked. Luke gazed up at her

through yellow eyes, all trace of his human per-
sonality hidden beneath the werewolf's exterior.

Cleo tore a strip of bandage from her waist
and hastily tied it around the wound on Luke's
leg. "It's not much, but it'll stop you from losing
blood."

The sound of clashing metal caught her attention, and she spun to see Resus backing across
the street, sword held high to fend off Sir Otto's
fierce blows. As he reached the curb, the vampire

stumbled and fell onto his back, twisting away just as the metal point of the man's weapon clanged into the concrete where his head had been seconds before.

Kicking out with a heavy boot, Sir Otto knocked the sword from Resus's hand. It skittered away across the wet pavement, leaving the vampire helpless. Cleo screamed in frustration and ran to her friend's aid.

A deep-throated growl rang out as the larger wolf leaped across the street. Luke jumped up a split second later, and the two beasts met in midair, snapping at each other with glistening fangs.

The air sizzled with electricity as another fork of lightning crackled in the sky. The intense light reflected off the wet fur of the wolves and lit them up, frozen for a moment like figures in some nightmarish photograph.

The creatures crashed back down to the ground, the smaller werewolf first to its feet. Jaws wide, it lunged for its opponent's exposed throat.

"Luke, no!" a familiar voice screamed, causing the werewolf's head to snap up. Two figures stood huddled together, soaked by the storm. The couple's expressions of terror could be seen clearly as another surge of white-hot lightning flashed above. The werewolf howled with rage to discover that his parents were watching him. . . .

Luke sat bolt upright, his T-shirt dripping from the pounding rain. No, it wasn't rain—it was sweat. He was lying on his bed, fully dressed.

Trying to slow his racing heartbeat, he switched on the lamp. The glow of the bulb reflected against the contours of a silver face embossed into the front of a book on his desk.

As Luke peeled off his dripping shirt and grabbed another from the drawer, the face opened its eyes. "You were dreaming again," it said.

"So what?" snapped Luke, pulling on the T-shirt. "Everyone has dreams."

"Very true," agreed the face calmly. "But not everyone transforms into a werewolf while doing so."

Luke followed the book's gaze and saw deep claw marks scratched into the closed bedroom door. His fingertips were bloodied, and he could see sharp splinters of wood in some of them. "Did I get out?" he asked. "My mom and dad . . ."

"They locked the door when they heard you shout in your sleep. They're perfectly safe."

Luke buried his head in his sore hands.

Samuel Skipstone, author of *Skipstone's Tales of Scream Street,* watched sadly from the front cover of his life's work. Casting a spell to merge his dying spirit with the pages of his book had meant that he could continue to research the residents of this unusual community long after his physical death, but it stopped him from being able to offer a comforting shoulder when required.

"Do you want to talk about your dream?" he asked.

"It's the same as always." Luke shrugged. "I'm out in the street, fighting another werewolf."

"Is anyone else there?"

"Cleo," said Luke. "And Resus is fighting Sir Otto." He stood and watched the rain batter against the windowpane for a few seconds. "What does it mean?"

"Perhaps you would be better off asking your vampire friend himself why he would want to battle with the landlord of Scream Street," suggested Skipstone.

Luke snorted back a laugh. "I can think of a hundred reasons why he would attack Sneer," he said. "Choosing just one would be difficult!"

Skipstone smiled. "Master Negative is not alone in his dislike of that man."

"My parents are watching the battle," continued Luke, "but I don't see them until I'm about to kill the other werewolf."

"I'm sure the dream represents nothing more than your reluctance for them to see you in your true form."

"True form?" said Luke. "This is my true form: a normal, everyday kid! That *thing* I become isn't me!"

"Lycanthropy has a long and noble history," said Samuel Skipstone. "Many families are proud of their werewolf tradition."

"Mine isn't!" said Luke. He thrust his injured fingers toward the silver face. *"This* is what my family thinks. They lock me away so I can't tear out their throats in their sleep." He sighed. "I need to wash my hands."

As Luke suspected, the bedroom door was still locked when he tried the handle. He hammered his fist against the damaged wood, trying not to look at the claw marks in the varnish. "Mom! Dad! Can you let me out now?"

A hastily whispered conversation took place on the other side of the door. "I'm not sure that's a good idea, Luke," replied his dad eventually. "It might be better if you stay in there until the morning."

"But I need to use the bathroom," said Luke.

"I put a bucket in the corner, by the desk," said Mrs. Watson, her trembling voice revealing her nervousness. "You can use that for tonight."

Luke turned away from the door, fighting the urge to kick it. "I've got to get out of here!" he muttered, reaching beneath his bed to slide out the glistening golden casket he kept there.

He opened the lid and checked that the two items he had hidden inside — a vampire's fang and a vial of witch's blood — were still there. These were the first of the relics left behind by Scream Street's founding fathers. Luke was on a quest to find all six artifacts: a collection that would give him the power to open a doorway back to his world and take his parents home.

"I don't see how you *can* get out of here," said Samuel Skipstone. "Your parents seem intent on keeping your bedroom locked."

Luke closed the casket and slid it back into the shadows beneath his bed. "There's more than one way out," he said.

He slipped his feet into his sneakers, then grabbed the silver book and pushed it into his backpack. He opened the window, briefly screwing his eyes shut against the driving rain, and clambered onto the window ledge. Weak moonlight shimmered off the wet bark of a tree that grew a few yards from the house. As Luke tried to make it out, he struggled to recall where the strongest branches were and which of the dark shapes were merely shadows.

Of Scream Street's many strange characteristics, the state of constant night was the one Luke found hardest to deal with.

"I hate it being dark all the time!"

"The sun was conjured away many years ago," said Skipstone from Luke's backback. "It remains a prisoner to this very day."

"Where?" asked Luke.

"Some say it is trapped right here in Scream Street," replied the author. "Others say it was tricked into shining on a mere imitation of our community. We may never know the truth."

"Just one more reason to leave, then," said Luke grimly. With a last glance back at the bucket in the corner of his room, he leaped out into the night.

Chapter Two
The Clue

"Hold still!" Cleo snapped. "I can't bandage your leg while you're pacing around the room like you've got bats in your pants!"

"What I don't get," said Resus as he rearranged items inside his cape, "is how you cut your shin if you were scratching at the door with your hands."

Luke reddened. "I fell out of the tree outside my bedroom window."

Cleo gave up on Luke's leg and grabbed a pair of tweezers from next to a candle on the dresser. The flame glinted off the golden artifacts that filled her bedroom. "Let me have a look at your hands, then."

"They think I'm a monster," said Luke as Cleo began to pluck the splinters from his fingertips. "Ouch!"

"Resus," Cleo said, "tell him his parents don't think he's a monster."

"Don't look at me," said Resus. "They think *I'm* a monster, and I'm as normal as they are!" He produced a pair of false fangs from inside his cape and clipped them over his own teeth. Born to vampire parents, Resus was something of an oddity in his family. He hated the taste of blood, resorted to dyeing his blond hair, and needed more than a little help in the fangs department.

Luke sighed and traced his now splinter-free fingers over the hieroglyphics etched into a golden box that stood against the wall.

"Now," said the mummy, "lean against my sarcophagus so I can tend to that cut on your leg. You don't want it getting infected."

"Lean against your *what*-agus?" asked Luke.

"My sarcophagus!" replied Cleo. "That thing you're rubbing. My bed."

Luke pulled his hand away and stared at the glittering casket. The engraving of a girl's face gazed back at him from its lid. "You sleep in this?"

"Of course," said Cleo, wrapping a clean bandage around the wound on Luke's leg. "I couldn't relax in one of those soft, girly things!"

As Cleo tied off the dressing, the door opened and a giant mummy entered, carrying a golden tray. Bandages covered the huge figure from head to toe. "Visitors to my home, you honor my daughter with your friendship," he said.

"There's no need to get all formal, Dad," said Cleo as she jumped up to relieve him of the tray. "What are these?"

"I present sweetmeats created from the flora that borders the mighty Nile," thundered the mummy before bowing awkwardly and backing out of the room.

"What's he talking about?" asked Resus.

Cleo sniffed at the snacks on the tray. "Lotus-flower fritters." She beamed, offering the tray around. "Delicious!"

Resus cautiously picked up one of the small cakes, holding it at arm's length as though it might poison him. "Your dad makes food out of plants?"

"What else do you think we vegetarians eat?" demanded the mummy.

"Well, not flowers!"

"Just because your family eats nothing but meat," teased Cleo.

"We do not just eat meat," retorted Resus. "We often have French fries as well."

Cleo threw a fritter to the vampire. "Try that," she said. "It tastes like beef."

Resus bit into the lotus-flower snack and

smiled. "Hey, you're right!" he said, stuffing the rest of it into his mouth. Some crumbs fell to the floor, and half a dozen small silver spiders skittered out from under the dresser to collect the tiny pieces in a webbing sack.

"What *is* it with them?" asked Resus as he watched the spiders work. "We don't need them now that we've got the electricity back." Having struggled with gas as their only source of power for years, the residents of Scream Street had trained spiders to clean their carpets and floors.

"They've seen me use the vacuum cleaner," said Cleo, "but they don't seem to want to stop helping. They appear under the table at every mealtime."

"My parents haven't eaten properly for two weeks," said Luke softly, "since we were brought to Scream Street."

"Then perhaps," announced a voice, "it is time to find the next relic." Luke pulled *Skipstone's Tales of Scream Street* from his backpack. "You already possess the vampire's fang and witch's blood," said the author. "With the third relic you will be halfway through your quest to take your parents home."

Samuel Skipstone closed his eyes, and the book flipped open to a page that contained a detailed recipe for dragon-scale soup. The words faded away to reveal a section of hidden text beneath:

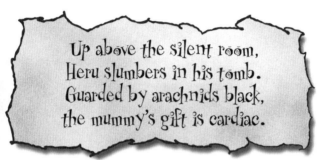

Up above the silent room,
Heru slumbers in his tomb.
Guarded by arachnids black,
the mummy's gift is cardiac.

"The next founding father is a mummy!" said Luke.

"And we have to go to his tomb," added Resus.

"We can't!" protested Cleo.

Luke turned to her in surprise. "We have to."

"You can't enter a mummy's tomb unin-vited," Cleo insisted, tears soaking into the bandages around her eyes. "It's how I lost my mom!"

"You've never mentioned your mom before," said Resus as he, Luke, and Cleo walked along Scream Street the next morning.

"I don't want to talk about it," said the mummy.

"I wondered why your dad was the only adult mummy on Scream Street," Resus continued bluntly. "Hey! Your daddy is really a mummy!"

Cleo grunted in frustration and sped up, marching ahead. "I only just got that," Resus said, beaming. "Cleo's daddy is a mummy!"

Luke looked nervously at Cleo, up ahead, then back to Resus. "I don't think—"

"How does he choose which bathroom to use?" The vampire giggled.

His smile vanished as Cleo spun to face him. "My mom's sarcophagus was washed overboard on the boat trip over here from Egypt, OK?"

"OK, OK," muttered Resus. Leaves rustled in the bushes behind them and Luke glanced around, but no one was there.

"My dad and I haven't seen her since, and it's all because some stupid explorers entered her tomb and took her coffin for their museum without an invitation!" snapped the mummy. "Now do you see why I don't want to break into this founding father's resting place?"

"I do," said Luke gently, "but if this mummy

17

agreed to leave behind a relic so that he could help others, isn't that sort of an invitation to visit him?"

"I suppose so." Cleo sighed. "I know I'm going to regret this, but which house are we going to?"

"There are a few empty houses, but number thirty-two has been vacant longer than any of the others," said Resus.

"And you think this mummy will have his tomb in there?" asked Luke.

"I think that's what Skipstone's clue meant," said Resus. "It said it was up above—"

He was interrupted by the sound of drums echoing along Scream Street.

"What is *that*?"

"I GUESS NUMBER THIRTY-TWO ISN'T EMPTY ANYMORE!" Luke shouted over the noise as he watched an army of men in purple jumpsuits carry boxes into the black brick house. None of the men had a single facial feature: no eyes, ears, nose, or mouth. Luke shivered as he recalled the moment the Movers had arrived at his own home to bring his family to Scream Street.

"Who do you think is moving in?" yelled Cleo.

"No idea!" bellowed Resus. "G.H.O.U.L. never gives us any warning." As he spoke, the air in front of the trio shimmered and a phantom materialized—a phantom with the wildest head of teased hair Luke had ever seen.

"Well, looky here." The ghost grinned, taking Resus's hand and shaking it hard. "Seems like we got ourselves some music fans!"

He gestured back toward the house. "I guess you recognize this here as Buddy Bones, the greatest skeleton jazz drummer in the world?"

"Which band did he play with?" asked Resus.

"Never went near another musician," said the ghost. "Hated them, in fact. So he always played alone. Fifteen albums of nothing but drum solos!"

"Sounds like—" began Cleo, but the phantom didn't wait for her to finish.

"Simon Howl," he said, pushing a translucent business card into Luke's palm. "President of Moantown Records."

Two of the Movers stumbled past, carrying an old-fashioned jukebox between them. "Now, you boys be careful with that," warned Simon. "That box contains some of the rarest records you're ever likely to come across."

The Movers gave no indication that they had heard the phantom speak. They set the jukebox down in the yard and went back for more items.

"What's the deal with these guys?" asked Simon. "I tried to tip 'em when they cleared out

 20

our old place, but they don't appear to hear a word I say!"

"They're from G.H.O.U.L.," explained Resus. "Government Housing of Unusual Life-forms. They've had all their senses removed so they can never accidentally reveal the location of Scream Street."

"*All* their senses?" asked the phantom.

Resus nodded. "All except their sense of touch, which they need to move your belongings from your old house to here."

"They can't even speak?" said Simon. "Man, it must be quiet where they live!"

Luke turned to face Resus and Cleo. "You could even say it would be silent. . . ." he said with a grin.

Chapter Three
The Attic

Cleo turned the ornate brass handle and pushed. The door to 5 Scream Street swung open. "It's unlocked!" she exclaimed.

"Shh!" warned Luke.

"I don't need to 'shh,'" said Cleo. "The Movers haven't got ears, remember? They can't hear what I'm saying."

"No, but they might be able to feel the vibrations of your speech in the air."

"That's right," added Resus. "My uncle Sisor was as blind as a vampire bat, and his other senses grew stronger to compensate. He could feel a drop of blood hitting the floor at a hundred yards."

"You two are just being ridiculous!" snapped Cleo. "If they could 'feel' my voice in the air, they'd have done something by n—"

She squealed as a pair of strong hands reached out of the darkness and pulled her into the house.

"After we save her," Resus said to Luke, "it's my turn to say 'I told you so'!"

The inside of the Movers' house was pitch-black. Luke felt his way slowly along one of the walls—until he cracked his shin against the edge of a low table.

"This is ridiculous," he hissed. "The Movers may not need light to see, but I'm helpless in the dark!"

 23

"Hang on a minute," whispered Resus. He reached into his cape and pulled out a flaming torch. The room lit up as the fire crackled.

"What are you doing?" demanded Luke. "The Movers would feel the heat from that a mile away!"

Resus sighed and pushed the torch back inside his cloak, fishing out a small, battery-operated flashlight instead. The beam did little to pierce the darkness, but it was better than nothing.

Staying close together, Luke and Resus stepped into the living room. Movers sat eerily still on the settee, their blank faces glowing as the flashlight beam flashed across them.

"Where's Cleo?" mouthed Luke. As Resus shrugged, a squeal from upstairs answered his question. Instantly the Movers in the room were on their feet and rushing toward the sound, expertly avoiding the furniture in their way.

Luke and Resus followed the men up the stairs and into a bedroom, where the Movers were crowding around a bed. The boys crept in behind them.

One of the Movers was tying Cleo's hands and feet to the bedposts with her own bandages.

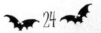 24

Resus started forward, but Luke held him back. "We can't risk spooking them," he said quietly. "We don't know how they'll react to us."

"We can't just leave her there!" hissed Resus.

"We'll get her out," said Luke, "but we'll have to wait for the right opportunity." The boys were flat against the wall to avoid bumping into anyone and revealing that they were there. Fortunately, Cleo's struggling seemed to mask the vibrations from their voices.

On some silent signal, each Mover raised his right hand and pressed his fingertips against the forehead of his nearest neighbor.

"That's how they communicate," said Resus as he and Luke slid into a gap beside the closet. "Some sort of telepathic vibration."

The boys watched as one of the Movers pressed a hand to the side of Cleo's face. The mummy's eyes snapped wide open, and she shouted, "Of course you can't feel a heartbeat, you idiot. My heart's in the fridge at home!"

"They're questioning her," whispered Resus. "She must be able to hear their voices inside her head!"

"Forget waiting for an opportunity," said Luke. "We have to stop this now. If she lets slip that we're here to find Heru's tomb, the Movers may tell Sir Otto where the next relic is."

Another shout from Cleo echoed around the room. "No, I'm not here to try to sell you vinyl siding!"

"We need a distraction," Resus said, pulling items from his cape: a scented candle, a bottle of vanilla flavoring, and a pair of sunglasses.

"Are you joking?" asked Luke. "These are no good—the Movers don't have any senses!"

"Stop hassling me," snapped Resus. "I'm trying to—aha!" The vampire grinned as he found what he was looking for.

"You've got to be kidding me," hissed Luke, staring at the collection of objects Resus was holding out.

"You're the one who said we need a distraction," said Resus defensively. "Unless you want blabber-bandages to talk, I suggest you put these on."

Luke sighed, handed Resus his backpack, and tied the two lengths of elastic around his knees as Resus swung a pair of leather straps over his

friend's shoulders and fastened the buckle. Then
Resus pulled a kazoo out of his cloak, pushed
it into Luke's mouth, and stood back to admire
Scream Street's first one-man band.

"Go on!" urged the vampire.

Luke glared at Resus, then began to stomp
toward the door, knocking his knees together to
clash the cymbals tied to them. With each step, the
bass drum on his back boomed. Sighing heavily,
Luke began to hum a rousing version of "When
the Saints Go Marching In" on the kazoo.

Resus fought the urge to
laugh as every Mover in
the room turned toward
Luke, the vibrations of
the dreadful music
flooding their
one and only
sense.

As Luke crashed
and banged his way
out the door, the
Movers instantly
forgot Cleo and
followed. Resus dashed

over to the bed and untied the bandages from the mummy's wrists and ankles.

"What's going on?" asked Cleo. One of the Movers stopped in the doorway, sensing the air moving as she spoke. Resus clamped a hand over the mummy's mouth and signaled for her to be quiet.

Resus led Cleo onto the tiny landing, where the Movers stumbled toward the deafening percussion sounds at the top of the stairs. Each held out his hands to find his way as his delicate sense of touch throbbed from the noise.

"What *is* Luke doing?" whispered Cleo.

Resus shone his flashlight on Luke to reveal him slipping the drum off his back and untying the cymbals from his knees, all the while making as much noise as he could. "He's about to have a smash hit!" the vampire said with a grin.

Luke tossed the instruments down the stairs and ducked to one side as the Movers followed the sounds all the way to the bottom. The bass drum crashed, and the cymbals bounced off the walls. As the last of the faceless men felt his way down the banister, Luke joined his friends on the now empty landing.

"Simon Howl could get you on the charts with that!" Resus laughed.

"Now what?" asked Cleo.

"We go *up,*" said Luke. "Mr. Skipstone said the mummy was *above* the silent rooms."

Resus shone the flashlight toward the ceiling and spotted a small attic hatch with a wooden ladder running up to it.

"I'll go first," said Cleo. She grabbed the rungs and began to climb.

As she pushed open the hatch and disappeared into the attic, Luke sighed. "Do you think we can leave her behind when we go to find the next relic?" he asked. "It's like trying to control a disobedient puppy."

"We'd better get up there before the Movers figure out they've been tricked and come looking for us," said Resus.

Luke took the flashlight and held it between his teeth as he climbed the ladder. As he entered the attic and the gloom was lifted by the dim light, he froze.

Cleo was caught in a giant spiderweb.

Chapter Four
The Mummy

Glossy dark spiders swarmed over Cleo, wrapping her in a cocoon of webbing as Luke and Resus clambered up into the attic.

"At least we know we're in the right place," said Luke. "They must be the *arachnids black* Mr. Skipstone warned would be guarding Heru's tomb."

"They're a lot bigger than the cleaning spiders," added Resus.

"I don't care how big they are," hissed Cleo. "Just get them off me!"

Luke sighed and grabbed the web holding Cleo captive. As he tore at the sticky substance, the spiders attacked, racing up his arm toward his face.

He yelled and pulled his hand away, shaking it to try to dislodge the creatures, but they had already begun to spin more webbing. The flashlight clattered to the ground, its beam casting dramatic shadows against the walls.

Within seconds, Luke's wrist was pinned to one of the beams that ran across the attic. The spiders moved on, scuttling across his shoulder and onto his cheek, their jaws constantly clicking. Luke could feel dozens of tiny legs pressing on his skin as his mouth became covered in a shimmering silver gag.

He tried to turn his head to see if Resus was

faring any better, but his hair was now fixed to the wooden beams. More and more of the deathly black spiders emerged from the shadows to spin their sticky thread across Luke's body. His legs were now completely encased in webbing, and it wouldn't be long before his arms fell to the same fate.

Luke was angry that they had been captured so easily, and he shuddered as a familiar feeling washed over his face. Bones splintered and broke, pushing outward and reforming. The muscles in his cheeks and jaw tore apart and knitted together again. Razor-sharp fangs pushed his own teeth out of place. This was one of the many partial transformations he had experienced since living in Scream Street.

His head now that of a werewolf, Luke pushed his long, rough tongue forward and used it to saw at the web over his face like a prisoner rasping at cell bars with a file. Once his mouth was free, Luke twisted his head around and bit at the webbing that bound his arms.

He banged his fist repeatedly against one of the wooden beams to rip it from the web, and for a second all the spiders stopped spinning and

turned to look at him. Once his arm was free, the creatures made a clicking sound and went back to work.

Scanning the attic for his friends, Luke saw Cleo struggling beneath layers of glistening gossamer. Resus's position wasn't much different. The vampire's body was wrapped in the web, and several dozen spiders were busy covering his face. As his eyes began to disappear, Luke saw Resus flick his gaze downward.

Luke swung to the side, tearing at the threads that bound his waist. He thrust his hand into the web around Resus and inside the vampire's cloak.

With a triumphant howl he pulled the flaming torch from his friend's cape and pushed it into the web around Cleo. The spiders clicked and skittered away as the silver cocoon began to dissolve, shrinking and twisting as it burned.

As Cleo's bandages began to reappear, Luke turned and began to work on Resus. The spiders kept their distance from the part-werewolf, eyes glistening in the flickering light.

When Resus had enough movement in his arms, he ripped the remaining webbing from his body and reached Cleo just as she fell to the floor.

 33

The mummy opened her eyes and forced a smile.

Luke burned the silk around his legs as his face slowly transformed back from werewolf to human. Once he was free, he lunged forward and plunged the flaming torch in among the cluster of spiders. They clicked madly, racing for the loft hatch and safety.

"Shouldn't we stop them?" asked Cleo as she climbed shakily to her feet. "They're supposed to be guarding Heru's resting place."

"You want to invite them *back*?" asked Resus. "Besides, there won't be anything left to guard once we have his heart."

"How do you know the relic is his heart?" asked Luke.

"It says so in the clue."

Luke pulled *Skipstone's Tales of Scream Street* from his backpack and held the torch over the page containing the clue.

Up above the silent room,
Heru slumbers in his tomb.
Guarded by arachnids black,
the mummy's gift is cardiac.

"*Cardiac* means relating to the heart and surrounding arteries," explained the vampire. "What?" he added as Luke and Cleo stared at him in disbelief. "There's nothing wrong with paying attention in class!"

"So," said Luke, "where *is* this mummy?" He held out the flaming torch as he clambered farther into the dingy attic.

Another large web blocked his path, and he melted it with the tip of the torch. As it disappeared, Luke found a pair of piercing eyes staring back at him. He jumped, tripped over a crate, and hit the floor with a crash. His foot tore away more of the webbing to reveal that the face was carved into the lid of a golden sarcophagus edged with hieroglyphics.

"Guys," he said, holding up the torch. "I think I've found it."

Resus stared at the golden figure. "Let's find the heart and get out of here before the Movers figure out that we're up here." He began to pull crates and boxes away from the sarcophagus.

Luke squeezed through the gap Resus had made and burned away the remaining spiderwebs. When he had finished, he wedged the torch

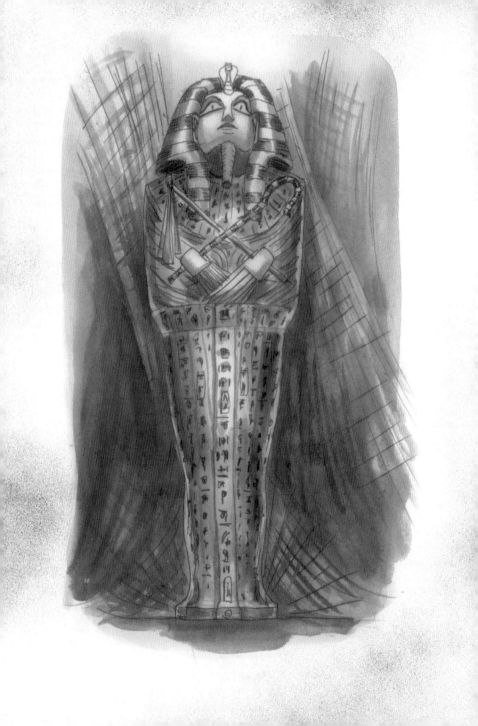

securely in one of the ceiling beams. "OK," he said. "Here goes!" He slid his fingers into the thin crack running along the side of the casket's lid and pulled hard. The sarcophagus began to open, creaking after years of neglect.

Cleo stepped in front of him and slammed the lid closed.

"What are you doing?" Luke protested.

"I'm sorry," she said. "I just can't let you do this!"

"I haven't got a choice," said Luke. "I need all six of the founding fathers' relics to open a doorway out of Scream Street."

"I understand that," said Cleo. "And I sympathize, I really do. But we can't just go rummaging around inside this sarcophagus! It might sound like silly superstition to you, but I believe in this stuff."

Resus sighed. "We've been through this," he said. "Heru left his heart behind to be used by someone who really needs it."

"I know," said Cleo.

"Then what's the problem?" demanded Luke.

"Heru was royalty."

"What? Royalty, as in a king or something?"

Cleo nodded. "He was a pharaoh."

Resus stared at her in amazement. "And you haven't mentioned that before now because . . . ?"

"I only just found out," explained Cleo. "The hieroglyphics say so."

Luke studied the symbols on the sarcophagus. "You can read these?"

"It's kindergarten stuff," said Cleo, indicating a series of images depicting a bowing man, a river, an eye, and an eagle. "These mean he was revered for his benevolence and wisdom. We must worship and adore him."

Resus giggled. "Are you sure?" he asked. "To me it looks more like he took underwater yoga lessons from a one-eyed crow!"

"Oh, really?" snapped Cleo. "And what does it mean in vampire culture when you have to wear false fangs because you're nothing but a normal?"

Luke sighed. "If you two have finished annoying each other, can we please open this box so that I can get the heart and go home?"

"But he's a pharaoh. . . ."

"Not anymore, he's not," said Resus. "He's lost property in a dusty attic."

"What if we bow down to him as the casket opens?" asked Luke, struggling to keep his own temper in check. "Would that be OK?"

"I s'pose," said Cleo.

"OK," he said, relieved. "On the floor and help me pull."

The trio dropped to their knees, eyes averted from the sarcophagus as they opened it. The lid thumped against the wall, producing a shower of dust that crackled as it hit the flame of the torch.

A pair of bandaged feet came into view. Then an imposing figure, still lost in the shadows, clambered to its feet.

Cleo nudged Luke.

"What?"

"Say something!" Cleo hissed.

"Why me?" whispered Luke, his eyes still averted from the figure before them.

"Because you're the one after his relic!"

"OK," Luke said, clearing his throat. "Er . . . What was his name again?"

"Heru," muttered Resus.

"That's the one!" said Luke. This wasn't going as well as he'd hoped. "Mighty Heru, we worship your greatness and ask for deliverance of the gift you bestowed upon Scream Street as a founding father. . . ."

Silence filled the attic as the words echoed away. Nothing happened for a moment, then a bandaged hand clamped down on Luke's shoulder and a voice shouted out, "You're it!"

Chapter Five
The Gift

Luke yawned. Accompanied by Resus and Cleo, he had been playing tag with the mighty Heru for the past half hour—even though the pharaoh insisted he couldn't be "it" because he had diplomatic immunity.

Resus slumped against the beam beside his friend. "I wonder if the hieroglyphics mention that he's about as mature as a four-year-old!"

Luke glanced over at Cleo, who was pretending to get her bandages caught on a nail so that the clapping Heru could escape her clutches.

"I haven't had this much fun since I ordered three hundred slaves to be whipped for laughing at my sandals," Heru said with a giggle, twirling his loose bandages.

Resus forced a smile. "Sounds wonderful, Your Majesty."

Heru clamped a hand over his mouth. "Say that again!" he exclaimed.

"What?" asked Resus.

"What you just said," insisted Heru. "Say it again!"

"What? 'Sounds wonderful, Your Majesty'?"

Heru spun to face Cleo, gasping. "Doesn't he sound just like Ramone, the telepathic cattle-herder from *The Nile Flows North*?"

"Er . . . What's *The Nile Flows North*?"

"Ancient Egypt's most popular soap opera," explained Cleo. "It was acted out live every afternoon in front of the pharaoh's temple."

 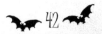

"And I would have been perfect for the role of Pyre, the slave-master's dashing half brother," said Heru with tears in his eyes. "But they just wouldn't give me an audition!" The mummy sobbed for a moment before bursting into a grin so wide it threatened to tear his bandages. "I know, I know, I know!" he shouted, jumping up and down on the spot. "Let's do the show right here!"

Luke smiled politely. "As tempting as your offer is, Your Majesty, I have to ask for the relic you agreed to leave behind as a founding father." He took a deep breath. "I need your heart."

"That old thing?" tutted Heru. "I got rid of that years ago!"

Luke stared at the mummy in disbelief. "You got rid of it?"

"Oh, yes," said Heru. "Far too ugly to give as a gift. I replaced it with this." The mummy pulled a small glass snow globe from inside his bandages and handed it to Luke. "I give you my new and improved relic!"

Luke gazed into the globe. Inside was a crude model of a spider, basking in bright sunlight.

"What's this?" he asked.

Heru shrugged. "No idea," he admitted. "I found it in one of the boxes up here. Pretty, though, isn't it?"

"Yes, Your Majesty," said Luke, trying to hide his irritation. "However, it's not much use to me. It's your heart that I need."

"But my heart doesn't look anywhere near as lovely as that," insisted Heru, tears filling his eyes once more.

Luke's patience was beginning to wear thin. "I don't *care* what it looks like!"

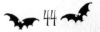

Cleo quickly stepped between Luke and the mummy, taking the snow globe in her hands. "I think it's beautiful, Your Majesty! Can I have it?"

"What are you doing?" hissed Luke.

"Play along or you'll never get his heart," Cleo whispered.

Heru wiped away his tears. "*You* want it?"

"I do, Your Majesty," said Cleo, pretending to be enraptured. "It's the most incredible thing I've ever seen. You have exquisite taste!"

A smile played across Heru's trembling lips. "I do, rather, don't I?"

Cleo nodded. "And I think you should punish this ungrateful wretch."

Heru clapped his hands in delight. "Ooh, I like punishing people! What shall I do? Throw him to the dogs? Tear him apart with horses?"

"Something worse," said Cleo.

Heru skipped around in a circle. "I could cut him open with a golden knife and fill his guts with scarab beetles!"

"Much too good for him, sire," Cleo said with a grin.

"Cleo . . ." muttered Luke.

"What?"

"Can we stop with the 'one hundred and one ways to torture Luke' thing, please?"

"Shh! Trust me." Cleo turned back to Heru. "I have a better idea, Your Majesty. Why not insist that he take your ugly old heart after all?"

"You think that would be a suitable punishment?"

"I do," said Cleo. "After all, he didn't appreciate this wondrous gift. Give him something disgusting instead. *Make* him accept it!"

Heru grinned wickedly. "It shall be done. Boy, my heart is yours to keep!"

Luke forced away his smile. "No, your Pharaoh-ness, please!"

Heru winked at Cleo. "My mind is made up," he said, "and it was all my own idea—nobody helped me with it at all. You *must* take my heart!"

"Oh, what a dreadful reward. I am undone with grief," Luke said flatly. He dropped to his knees and held out his hands. "Hand me the punishment I most truly deserve!"

"What?"

"Your heart," said Luke. "You were going on about it just now . . ."

"Oh, my heart's not here," said Heru. "It's in a golden casket at the bottom of the square river."

Luke stared. All this, and the heart wasn't even here!

Heru, however, was indifferent. He waved a bored hand toward Cleo. "Right, back to our play," he said. "You can bring me my wine, and when it's not cold enough, I'll have you whipped."

"An excellent idea," Cleo said, beaming. "Now, why don't you step back into your sarcophagus for a moment so you can make an entrance worthy of a pharaoh?"

Heru looked as though he might faint with excitement. "What a wonderful plan!" he squealed, stepping back inside his coffin. "Ooh, I'm a star! I'm a star!"

Cleo swung the lid closed and the attic was silent once more. "At last," she groaned. "Now, let's go and find his heart!"

Resus smirked. "You're locking the mummy back up? What about all that 'we must worship and adore him' stuff?"

"That," said Cleo with a deep sigh, "was before I knew he was crazier than a bucket of pencils!"

Luke, Resus, and Cleo raced out of 5 Scream Street, leaving the Movers chasing a chattering wind-up monkey around the house. "I knew that toy would come in handy one day!" the vampire said with a grin. "I've got another one somewhere."

"Hang on," said Luke. "If you had that monkey in your cloak all along, why did I have to stomp around as a one-man band to get us into the attic?"

Resus grinned. "That musical stuff's been weighing me down for weeks," he said. "I was glad to get rid of it!"

"And you *were* very entertaining," added Cleo.

Luke tried to look annoyed. "I should throw you two back to the Movers."

"Oh, yeah?" said Cleo. "Then who's going to help you find this 'square river,' whatever that is?"

"So Heru definitely said his heart was in a

casket at the bottom of a square river?" asked Luke. "I was hoping I'd heard wrong."

"What do you think he was talking about?" said Cleo.

A smile began to creep across Resus's face as an idea struck him. "Follow me," he said, running toward a garden on the opposite side of Scream Street.

Moments later, Luke found himself staring into a tank of filthy swirling water, surrounded on all sides by mud and overgrown reeds.

"Of course, technically it's more of a rectangle than a square. . . ." said Resus.

"What *is* that?" asked Luke as a series of gloopy green bubbles popped across the surface.

"Isn't it obvious?" replied Resus. "It's a swimming pool."

Luke stared at him. "Surely no one has a swimming pool like this!"

"Mr. and Mrs. Crudley do," Resus said.

"And Heru's heart is at the bottom?"

"Someone's coming!" hissed Cleo, pulling the boys down behind a compost heap that dominated one side of the garden. Luke pinched his nose and watched as a pulsating mound of something brown slithered out of the house, putting on an orange armband festooned with cartoon characters as it did so.

"What," whispered Luke, "is *that?*"

"A bog monster," replied Resus. "I take it you haven't met the Crudleys."

"I have, though," announced Cleo, jumping to her feet. "Fifi!"

With a scream that sounded like a whale breaking wind in an ocean of whipped cream, the bog monster jumped with fright and toppled into the pool. It thrashed about for a few seconds, then vanished beneath the rancid water.

A much larger, obviously angry bog monster oozed out the back door and glared at Cleo. "What have you done to my baby?" demanded Mrs. Crudley.

Fifi's head broke the surface again, and a mouth the size of an armchair gasped for breath.

"Keep kicking, darling," screamed her mother, racing up and down beside the pool, leaving a sticky trail of mud. "Somebody will save you!"

"I'll do it!" yelled Cleo. She thrust the snow globe into Resus's hands and dived into the

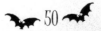

churning green cesspool. Within seconds the dirty water had soaked into her bandages, and she, too, was being pulled beneath the surface. She screamed through a mouthful of goo.

Luke and Resus looked at each other.

"I could have told you that would happen," the vampire said with a sigh as the two boys leaped headfirst into the pool of bubbling slime.

Chapter Six
The Heart

"**I still don't understand** why you have a swimming pool if none of you can swim," said Resus as he dried his hair with a very rough towel provided by Mrs. Crudley. Fifi was now sitting happily in a high chair made from steel, playing with a lump of soil the size of a small car.

Mr. Crudley oozed across the living room, a dark stain glistening on the carpet behind him.

"It adds to the value of the property," he said with a sniff, snatching a picture of Fifi from Cleo's hands and rubbing at the wooden frame with his muddy fingers.

"Please," he begged, "I must ask you not to touch anything. Children are such messy creatures, and we're very proud of our home!"

Cleo stared at the lumpy black mess now dripping over the photograph and stifled a laugh. "Of course, Mr. Crudley," she said.

"There was no sign of Heru's heart down there, though," Luke said, sighing. "Just gallons of slime."

"And not just *any* slime," boasted Mrs. Crudley as she took the towel from Resus and ran her hand proudly over the goo that coated it. "This slime was imported directly from an unexplored tributary to the Amazon River!" She sucked the green mess from her fingers and smiled.

"If it's unexplored," said Resus, "who went up there to get it for you?" Cleo busily rearranged the bandages on her face in an effort to disguise another laugh as Mrs. Crudley oozed across the room.

"Was there ever a golden casket at the bottom

of your swimming pool?" Luke asked the nearest mound of brown gunk, hoping he was looking at its face.

"Yes," gurgled Mr. Crudley. "Disgusting shiny thing. I put it in the cellar."

Luke cleared his throat. "Do you think we could see it?"

"*If* you stand on newspaper!" screeched Mrs. Crudley as she led Luke, Resus, and Cleo toward the cellar door. "And I'm only doing this because you saved my darling Fifi!"

A thick trail of slime seeped from the bottom of the bog monster as she slithered across the carpet, laying down pages from the *Terror Times* for Luke, Resus, and Cleo to stand on.

Luke went to open the cellar door, but Mrs. Crudley slapped his hand away. "Children have sticky fingers!" she snapped as she turned the handle, leaving behind tendrils of dripping slime. The stairway down to the basement was steep and vanished into menacing darkness. Luke led the way down.

Once Mrs. Crudley had left them, Resus pulled the flaming torch from his cloak, lighting the rest of the stairway. "I didn't think she'd appreciate the fire near her precious Fifi!" he said, grinning.

Luke climbed down the remaining stairs and studied the cramped cellar. Piles of furniture, carpets, and boxes filled every available space.

"Last season's styles," said Cleo. "The Crudleys are very fussy when it comes to keeping up with the latest fashions."

It took the trio almost an hour of shifting sofas and moving dining tables to locate the golden box. Eventually Cleo found it near a mound of disturbed earth in the corner. She dragged the casket to the center of the room.

"Ready?" asked Luke.

"Ready," confirmed Resus.

Holding his breath, Luke opened the lid of Heru's golden casket. Inside was a slip of torn paper containing just a few words in scrawled handwriting.

Luke read the message aloud. *"Dude, IOU one heart!"*

"You're sure it's Doug who took the heart?" asked Luke as they stepped out onto the Crudleys' front lawn.

Resus examined the note again. "Well, it's written in blood, so it's definitely a zombie, and there's only one I know of who speaks like that."

"Like what?" asked Cleo as Resus pulled a bottle of strong lager from his cloak and opened it with a *psst*.

"Dude!" said a muffled voice. A decayed green hand shot out of the grass and grabbed the bottle. As the hole widened, a scabby face appeared. "You sure know the way to a zombie's heart, little vampire dude."

"I was hoping you'd say that," Resus said, smiling, as Doug drank the beer. He held up the bloody note. "Was this you?"

"Guilty as charged," admitted the zombie.

"How?" asked Luke. "It took us ages to convince Mrs. Crudley to let us search the cellar, and even then we weren't sure we'd find it."

Doug tapped the side of his nose, dislodging it in the process and causing it to fall off into the dirt. "Never fails me," said the zombie as he spat on the back of the nose and pressed it noisily back in place. "I can smell a human organ at a hundred yards!"

"And the bog monsters just let you go down there and get it?"

"I don't mess with old man Crudley," said Doug. "He can produce sludge that'll just burn the skin right off you!" The zombie shook his head. "No, I tunneled into their cellar in the dead of night."

"But why do you need the heart?" asked Cleo.

"I'm cooking Sunday lunch for Turf and Berry this weekend," said Doug. "That juicy heart will taste righteous with roasted eyeballs on the side."

Cleo clamped a hand over her mouth. "You're going to *eat* it?"

"No, Cleo," said Resus sarcastically. "He's going to staple it to a piece of paper and make a Valentine with it."

"Berry loves a bit of heart," continued Doug. "She's been saving a bottle of spinal fluid for this weekend, too."

"Special occasion?" asked Resus.

 57

The zombie nodded. "It's Turf's re-birthday. Exactly thirty-eight years since he burst out of his grave and joined the undead."

"I know it's an important day," said Luke, "but I need that heart to help get my parents home."

"You can't take our heart, dude," protested Doug. "It's a celebration!"

"What if we found you something to replace it with?" said Resus. "A nice juicy stomach, perhaps, or a plump gallbladder?"

Cleo whimpered, grabbed the vampire's cloak, and clamped it over her mouth. Resus glared at the sweating mummy and yanked it back. "You're not helping here!" he hissed.

Doug paused to consider the offer, lifting off the top of his head to scratch his brain as he did so. Jamming

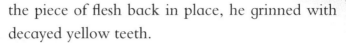

the piece of flesh back in place, he grinned with decayed yellow teeth.

"OK, little dudes," he said. "In the spirit of harmony, if you can find us a replacement main course, the heart is yours!"

Doug drained the last of the beer as Luke, Resus, and Cleo climbed to their feet. The zombie dipped his hand into the pocket of his filthy shirt and produced a handful of crisp brown curls. "Deep-fried finger before you go?"

"It's really not very polite to throw up *on* a zombie," said Resus as he, Luke, and Cleo emerged from the garden into Scream Street.

"Not polite?" demanded Cleo. "He offered us human flesh to eat!"

"And more to the point, you offered him something to replace the heart," said Luke, turning to Resus. "What did you have in mind?"

The vampire shrugged. "I dunno."

"You don't know?" exclaimed Luke in surprise. "I thought at the very least you'd have an elderly relative's liver tucked away inside your cloak!"

Resus shook his head. "My mom made me

bury them all after my bedroom was invaded by maggots."

Cleo paled again and clutched at a nearby garden gate for support. "It's at times like this I'm glad I'm a vegetarian," she groaned.

"That's it!" said Luke. "We'll get the zombies a vegetable replacement."

"I don't think that's a good idea," said Resus. "I talked Turf into trying a carrot once, and he went on a crazed rampage once he found out it hadn't come from something that used to breathe."

"So let's not tell them what it is," suggested Luke.

"You don't think they'll notice if they're eating a turnip instead of a heart?" asked Cleo.

"You said last night that your dad's lotus-flower fritters taste like beef," said Luke. "What else has he got in the fridge?"

"There's a mushroom and dandelion casserole," Cleo said thoughtfully, a smile beginning to show between her bandages. "And that tastes just like pork. . . ."

"Brilliant." Resus grinned. "We can soak it in blood from the tap and tell the zombies it's a gallbladder or something."

The trio arrived at Cleo's front gate, and the mummy raced up the path and pushed open the door. She ran to the kitchen and began to rifle through the fridge. Her father appeared.

"Dad, we need to—"

Cleo froze as she saw that the bandages over his face were soaked with tears. "What's wrong?"

"Hello, Cleo," came a voice from behind her father.

Cleo turned to stare at the female mummy standing in the kitchen doorway.

"Mom?" she whispered before everything went black and she fainted.

Chapter Seven
The Reunion

Resus and Luke dashed out of the zombies' house. "I have to admit, I'm amazed that that worked," said the vampire, clutching Heru's heart in his hands. "I was sure they'd notice that mushroom casserole was a vegetable dish."

"What? After you poured an entire jug of

blood over it?" Luke grinned. "I've got no idea what a gallbladder tastes like—and I hope I never have to find out—but I'm sure that much blood could mask the flavor of just about anything."

"What a house, though!" said Resus. "Did you see the zombies' furniture? I never would have thought you could make a sofa and loveseat out of body parts."

"And the deep-pile carpets," said Luke. "How can they afford stuff like that?"

Resus shrugged. "Human hair's pretty cheap if you raid graves and harvest it yourself." The vampire grinned. "Cleo would have puked everywhere!"

Luke sighed. "It didn't feel right, getting the heart without her," he said. "She did so much to convince Heru to give it to me."

"She's got other stuff to concentrate on at the moment," Resus pointed out. Luke nodded, and the boys walked in silence for a few minutes.

"You think that's really her mom?" he asked.

Resus frowned. "Why wouldn't it be?"

"I don't know," admitted Luke. "One minute she's telling us about her mom for the first time, and the next minute she's there, as large as life."

"Yeah," Resus said. "Sounds like the plot to Heru's soap opera."

"Sounds more like a massive coincidence to me."

"You're in Scream Street," said Resus. "Coincidence is a way of life here!"

"Hmm," muttered Luke.

"Look, if it'll make you feel any better, let's go in and show Cleo the heart," said Resus, handing over the relic. "That way you can thank her for helping out and it will put your mind at rest about her mom."

As the boys turned down the street that led to Cleo's house, Luke pushed Heru's heart deep into his backpack. Something about this just didn't feel right.

"After my sarcophagus was washed overboard, I spent almost five hundred years at the bottom of the ocean before sharks finally broke through the casket and dragged me out for food. . . ."

Resus grinned as Cleo's mother continued the story of her arrival in Scream Street. "I think we've found out where Cleo gets her luck from," he said.

64

"Excuse me,
Mrs. Farr . . ."
began Luke.

"Please,
dear, call me
Alexandria!"

"OK,"
said Luke,
"Alexandria . . .
If sharks
attacked your
sarcophagus,
why didn't
they eat you?"

The mummy tugged
at the bandages around her stomach. "No flesh,
darling," she explained. "I was mummified a
long time ago, and I'm all skin and bones under
here!"

The door opened, and Niles Farr entered with
a tray of drinks. Alexandria accepted a golden
goblet and took a sip before continuing. "After a
few nips, the sharks left me alone, and I floated
aimlessly until I became entangled in a fishing net
and was dragged back to shore."

"Where did you land?" asked Cleo, captivated.

"Somewhere on the east coast of Africa, I believe," said Alexandria. "Wherever it was, the sun was hot enough to dry out my bandages and I started walking." She sighed heavily. "It has taken me many, many years to finally reach Scream Street and my long-lost family!"

Niles wrapped his arm around his wife's shoulders, hugging her tightly. Cleo gazed fondly up at him.

"I don't get it," said Luke. "I thought only the Movers knew how to get to Scream Street."

"The secret of Scream Street's location can be found if you are prepared to look hard enough," replied Alexandria.

"That's not what Mr. Skipstone says," countered Luke, "and he should know—he's been researching this place for years."

"Excuse us!" interrupted Resus, grabbing Luke's arm and dragging him to the other side of the room. When they were out of earshot, he turned to his friend. "What do you think you're doing?"

"This isn't right," said Luke, glancing over

as the three mummies embraced one another. "That's *not* Cleo's mom."

"How can you say that?" snapped Resus. "Cleo and her dad seem to think she's the genuine article, and they should know."

"They're being fooled!" replied Luke. "They want to believe it's her so badly that they're overlooking the mistakes in her story."

"There's only been one mistake," said Resus, "and that was bringing you here! Now, show Cleo the heart and then we can leave the family alone to catch up."

"OK," Luke said with a sigh. He pulled Heru's heart from his pocket and took it over to where Cleo and her parents were sitting.

"We, er . . . have to go now," he said. "But I thought you'd want to see that we finally got the heart."

"Thank goodness," said Cleo. "That's three relics now, and—"

"Where did you get that?" interrupted Alexandria.

Luke stared at Cleo's mother. "A mummy gave it to us."

"Which mummy?"

"Heru," replied Luke. "He was a pharaoh."

"I know who Heru was," said Alexandria sternly. "I was an important member of his court before I met Niles and settled down to start a family."

Luke tried to force a smile, but a bad feeling was beginning to creep over him. "He's quite a character, isn't he?"

"I was present at his mummification, which is how I recognized his heart," said Alexandria. She put down her goblet of wine. "Hand it over."

"What?" asked Luke. "You can't be serious!"

"I am perfectly serious," snapped Alexandria. "A pharaoh's heart is not a souvenir to be collected, young man. Now, give it to me and I will see that it is returned to its proper resting place."

"Mom, you don't understand," began Cleo. "Heru gave Luke his heart to—"

"SILENCE!" commanded Alexandria. "I see that several centuries in your father's care have not improved your behavior, young lady. I shall deal with you once this thief has left our home."

"I am not a thief," exclaimed Luke indignantly. "This is mine!"

 68

Alexandria stood up. "Not anymore!" she bellowed, snatching the heart from his hands.

"No," said Luke, "you don't understand. . . ."

"Oh, I understand perfectly," replied Alexandria. "You're the new boy in Scream Street, trying to make your mark by stealing from those who are kind enough to accept you as one of their own."

"What?" asked Luke. "How do you know I've only just moved—"

"Well, it stops now," insisted Alexandria. "And once this has been returned to its rightful owner, I shall see that the other items you have taken are also confiscated from you."

"Give that back!" roared Luke, lunging for the mummy. He grabbed the bandages at the back of her head and pulled hard. Alexandria screamed.

"Mom!" squealed Cleo.

"Don't be stupid," said Resus, dragging Luke away from the mummy.

"Give me the heart!" shouted Luke. "Cleo, she's not your mom!"

"Stop it!" Cleo sobbed, throwing her arms around Alexandria and kicking out at Luke. "Stop it now!"

 69

"Luke, get off her," Resus shouted.

"I need that heart!"

A giant hand gripped Luke's shoulders and lifted him into the air. Niles Farr's face filled Luke's vision. "You have dishonored my family and my home," he growled.

Luke grabbed the bandages on Niles's face and pulled them down over his eyes. As the large mummy released his grip to adjust them, Luke dashed over to Cleo. "Something's not right," he insisted, pointing to Alexandria. "Don't trust that woman."

"Luke," pleaded Cleo, tears filling her eyes. "Stop this!"

"Get that horrid young man out of my house," roared Alexandria.

Niles grabbed Luke's ear and dragged him from the room. The huge mummy pulled open the front door and hurled Luke onto the lawn. "Stay away from my family!"

Luke jumped to his feet and reached the door just as Niles slammed it shut. "No," he yelled, hammering it with his fists. "Please. I need that heart to take my parents home. They can't stay here!"

Luke tried to catch his breath. He *couldn't* be wrong. That *couldn't* really be Cleo's mom. But whoever she was, she had possession of Heru's heart—leaving Luke without the relic, or his friends.

Chapter Eight
The Invasion

"I don't get it," said Luke, flopping onto his bed. "I thought Resus would have backed me up at least, but he seemed as angry as the rest of them."

"He and Miss Farr have known each other for a long time, haven't they?" asked Samuel Skipstone from the cover of his book.

Luke shrugged. "I guess so."

"Then it is likely he was just protecting his friend," said the author.

"Even if she's being fooled by someone pretending to be her mom?"

"Then you're certain she isn't who she claims to be?" asked Skipstone.

"Oh, I don't know," groaned Luke. "What do you think?"

"It was difficult for me to hear from the confines of your backpack," said Skipstone, "but the others seem to think she is genuine."

"They've been tricked!" insisted Luke.

"How can you be sure?"

Luke lay back and stared up at the ceiling. "Her story doesn't make sense. She said she spent centuries at the bottom of the ocean, for one."

"Continue," encouraged the author.

"She claims to have found a way into Scream Street by herself," said Luke. "You told me that the only way in or out is either by the Movers or by collecting the founding fathers' relics." He sighed. "It just doesn't add up."

"You remind me of myself at your age," Skipstone said with a smile.

"What do you mean?"

"I was once like you, Luke Watson," said Skipstone. "I found inconsistencies in people's stories and fought to discover the truth. It's what made me write articles such as this." The book opened and flicked through some pages before stopping at a handwritten essay accompanied by crude illustrations.

Luke stared at the title in the dim light. "*Top 25 Uses for Bat Poo?*"

"Oh, I'm sorry," said Skipstone. "Wrong page!" The book turned itself to another article.

Luke squinted at the tiny writing. "I don't know how anyone can read in this light," he moaned. "And I'm sure it's getting darker as I speak."

"You may be right," said Skipstone, the book closing as the author peered up at the window.

"It's this constant night," continued Luke. "Resus says I'll get used to it, but I don't know how long it'll take."

Skipstone's eyes widened in alarm. "This is not a natural darkness. . . ."

Luke jumped to his feet and dashed to the bedroom window. Instead of being able to look

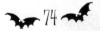

out over Scream Street below, all he could see was his own reflection. Something was obscuring his view. It looked like strands of . . .

"The spiders!" he exclaimed.

A scream rang out.

Luke pushed at the door to the living room, but it wouldn't open. By forcing against it with all his might he could see fine lines of webbing stretched between the door and its frame. The spiders were inside the house.

Luke's mom screamed again, her voice more muffled this time. Luke knew he had to get to her quickly, before she became completely cocooned by the spiders' silky gossamer webbing.

Luke took a few steps back and threw himself at the door, crying out in pain as his shoulder slammed against the hard wood. He heard footsteps and turned to see his father rushing along the hallway.

"Susan!" yelled Mr. Watson as he pounded his fists against the door. He spun to face Luke. "You have to get us in there!" he pleaded.

"I can't," said Luke, knowing what his dad meant. "Not in front of you."

"You have to!" shouted Mr. Watson, grabbing his son's shoulders. "Please!"

Luke trembled. The only time he had ever changed into his werewolf form in front of his father had been the very first time he had transformed. Working late, as he always did, Mr. Watson had missed his son's birthday party. Luke had been so angry that, when his dad finally arrived home, the wolf had taken over and he had attacked his own parents. If they hadn't managed to tie him up with bedsheets . . .

"I can't," said Luke. "What if I can't control it and go for *you*?"

Mr. Watson stared deep into his son's eyes. "That's a risk I'm willing to take," he said. "A risk we *have* to take."

Luke took a deep breath and closed his eyes. He pictured his mom trapped in a web as hundreds of shiny black spiders crawled over her, wrapping her in sticky thread. Soon her face would be completely covered and she wouldn't be able to breathe.

Rage pulsed through Luke, and he forced it down his arms,

toward his fingertips. He felt the bones in his fingers stretch and crack as thick claws burst through his skin. This time only his arms were changing.

Luke heard his dad gasp in terror, but he knew he couldn't allow himself to be distracted. Every second counted, and it could already be too late.

Finally, fur sprouted to cover Luke's strong paws. He opened his eyes and turned to the door. His first punch splintered the wood as though it were Styrofoam. Pulling free, he attacked again.

Soon Luke was able to tear apart what remained of the door. Long strands of webbing broke away as he ripped at the broken wood, creating a space big enough for him and his dad to squeeze through.

Everything in the room was covered in spiderwebs. Hundreds, if not thousands, of the tiny creatures skittered across every surface.

In the corner, suspended from the ceiling, Mrs. Watson was wrapped in webbing. Luke ran to her and began to tear at it, but as quickly as he could rip away

the web, more spiders appeared to replace it.

"Fire!" he shouted, turning to his dad. "I need fire!"

Mr. Watson scanned the room for something he could use to create a flame: a lighter or a box of matches. There was nothing.

Luke snatched *Skipstone's Tales of Scream Street* from his backpack. "What can I do?" he asked the silver face in panic. "I've got no way of burning them!"

"Try communicating with them," suggested Skipstone.

"Communicating?" demanded Luke. "How?"

"Have you tried talking to the spiders?"

Luke glanced up at the struggling shape of his mother. "No," he roared. "It might surprise you that I hadn't considered this the best time for a chat!"

"The spiders talk to one another by making a series of clicks," Skipstone explained, ignoring Luke's sarcasm. "If you can tap out a rhythm that means something in their language, you may be able to control them."

Luke suddenly remembered something. "Back in the attic, the spiders stopped spinning their webs when I banged my fist against the beams," he said thoughtfully.

"Can you recall the sequence of beats you used?"

"My mind's gone blank," said Luke despairingly. "I can't think!"

"Just try," suggested Skipstone. "I'm certain you can remember it if you try."

Luke turned the silver book over and tapped on the back with his long werewolf claws. *Tap, tap, tap, tap.* Nothing happened.

"It's not working!"

"Concentrate," said the author. "Picture yourself back in the attic."

Luke closed his eyes and imagined his fist banging against the wooden beam. He tapped again. *Tap, tap, tappity-tappity-tap.*

All over the room, spiders turned toward Luke, their slavering jaws clicking.

"Keep going," encouraged Mr. Watson. "It's working!"

Luke beat out the rhythm again, this time walking toward the broken door.

Tap, tap, tappity-tappity-tap.

As Luke climbed through the hole in the door,

a river of spiders began to follow him. Mr. Watson took the opportunity to rip at the silver threads enveloping his wife, tearing the webbing away from her face so she could gasp for air.

Tap, tap, tappity-tappity-tap.

Thousands of tiny feet skittered across the wooden floor of the hallway as Luke reached the front door. From the darkness beneath the kitchen table, dozens of the smaller cleaning spiders watched as their larger relatives marched to the beat of Luke's fingers.

Tap, tap, tappity-tappity-tap.

Luke led the entranced spiders out through the front door and into the street.

Tap, tap, tappity-tappit—

"What's wrong?" demanded Skipstone. "Why have you stopped?"

Luke turned the book over so that the author could see Scream Street for himself. Millions and millions of shimmering black spiders swarmed across the street, their thick webs stretching as far as the eye could see.

Luke swallowed hard. "We're going to need a bigger beat."

Chapter Nine
The Parade

Alexandria Farr turned the mummy's heart over in her bandaged hands. "What did that vulgar boy ever want with this?"

"It's one of six relics he needs to collect," explained Cleo. "Whoever possesses them all can make his greatest wish come true."

Resus shifted uncomfortably in his seat. "Cleo, I don't think . . ."

"It's OK," said Cleo. "I won't tell anyone

other than my mom." She smiled up at the older mummy and continued. "Luke wants to open a doorway out of Scream Street and take his parents home. They're terrified!"

"I see," said Alexandria, stroking her daughter's head. "And how many of these relics does he have already?"

Boom! Boom! Boom-ba-boom-ba-boom!

"Three so far," replied Cleo. "A vampire's fang, the blood of the first witch ever to live on Scream Street, and now this."

Boom! Boom! Boom-ba-boom-ba-boom!

"He keeps them in a casket under—"

"Cleo!" snapped Resus.

"What's the matter with you?" she asked.

Boom! Boom! Boom-ba-boom-ba-boom!

"And what *is* that dreadful noise?" demanded Alexandria, marching to the front door. It wouldn't open. "Niles, open this door!" she commanded.

Boom! Boom! Boom-ba-boom-ba-boom!

Cleo and her father joined Alexandria at the door. They all pushed against it, but the door would open only a few inches.

"It's a spiderweb!" Cleo gasped. She grabbed

a candle and thrust the flame into the webbing. It shriveled back, freeing the door and sending the three mummies tumbling out into the front yard.

Boom! Boom! Boom-ba-boom-ba-boom!

At last they could see what was causing the noise. Luke was stomping around Scream Street, once more strapped into the one-man band equipment, a legion of spiders trailing after him. The heavy bass drum on his back thumped with every step.

Boom! Boom! Boom-ba-boom-ba-boom!

"What in Dracula's name are you doing?" shouted Resus.

"Keeping the spiders busy!" yelled Luke. "Get everyone out of their houses so we can check that no one is left trapped in a web!"

Resus pulled the flaming torch out of his cape and raced down the street, closely followed by Cleo. Together they stopped at each house in turn, burning away the webbing that covered the front doors and then locating the residents.

Before long, occupants of Scream Street began to line the sidewalks, watching in amazement as Luke continued to lead the spiders away from their homes like a pounding Pied Piper.

Spiders crawled into the central square from each of the eight side roads that led away from it. Luke circled the square, constantly banging the drum so as not to end the rhythm.

Other residents took the lead from Resus. Tearing lengths of wood from door frames and fences, they lit them and scurried away to burn the webbing and check on their neighbors. Soon Scream Street was lit by the flickering of dozens of flaming torches.

Luke was just beginning to tire when Resus and Cleo finally reappeared from one of the side streets.

"Is everybody safe?" he yelled.

"Yes," bellowed Resus. "Everyone's accounted for!"

"OK," called Luke as he boomed on the spot. "I'll lead the spiders back to the Movers' attic. We'd better be quick. I think it's going to rain any min—"

A silver sword suddenly flew through the air and tore the skin of the bass drum, sending Luke toppling to the ground. There was silence.

Instantly the millions of spiders became aware that they were out in the open. Clicking their jaws in fear, they ran for cover.

The residents of Scream Street panicked and ran too, desperately trying to escape from the stampeding spiders. Hundreds of the shiny creatures were crushed underfoot—or, in the case of the Crudley family, slimed under goo.

Resus ran across the square to Luke and released the straps that held the bass drum to his back. "You OK?" he asked.

A shadow fell over the pair as Sir Otto Sneer reached down to retrieve the sword he had thrown.

"You!" hissed Luke.

"Who else?" Sir Otto said with a grin, puffing on one of his noxious cigars. "You see a plague of spiders; I see an opportunity to bring Scream Street to its knees!"

"But I was trying to save everyone," said Luke, shielding his eyes as drops of rain began to fall from the black clouds above. "Including you!"

Sir Otto rested on the hilt of his sword and adjusted the scarf that covered his throat. Luke shuddered as he caught a glimpse of the damaged flesh beneath—the result of an attack the landlord had suffered as a child. "I have a fondness for spiders," said Sir Otto. "I especially like their webs."

"They'll cover every inch of Scream Street!" said Resus.

"Not all of it," growled the landlord. "If I confiscate anything that can be used to make that rhythm and keep it playing around my grounds, Sneer Hall should remain web-free. *I'll* be fine. . . ."

Unable to listen any longer, Luke jumped to his feet and lunged for Sir Otto. He froze as the point of the landlord's sword pressed against his chest, glistening in the rain. "I wouldn't do that," the landlord said. "Werewolf or no werewolf, I'm pretty sure a blade can cause even *you* a lot of damage. . . ."

Luke took a step back as Sir Otto turned to face the only other people left in the square: Resus, Cleo, and Cleo's parents. "Now," he said, "to conclude my business here . . . Alexandria, give me Heru's relic."

"Never!" screamed Cleo. "My mom will never give you anything!" She flung her arms around her mother and pressed her face to her chest, feeling the soft heartbeat through her bandages.

Cleo's expression fell. She took a step away from the mummy. "I—I can hear your heart," she stammered.

"So?" demanded Alexandria.

"But mummies have their hearts removed before they're buried."

Alexandria Farr giggled. "You got me!" With a sound like a rippling stream, the mummy

transformed back into Sir Otto's shape-changing nephew, Dixon.

Cleo froze in horror. "Luke was right," she sobbed. "You aren't my mom!"

"No, he isn't," announced Sir Otto as he crossed the square toward the group. "Good disguise, though, don't you think? And he didn't do too badly with the backstory!" Dixon smiled at the rare praise from his uncle. A fork of lightning arced across the sky as the rain increased.

"You have deceived my family!" roared Niles Farr, rushing at Sir Otto with his fists clenched. Sir Otto quickly swung his sword around, and the large mummy ran into it, the blade piercing his stomach.

Luke and Resus raced over as Niles fell to the wet ground.

"Dad!" screamed Cleo, dropping to her knees beside her father.

"Oh, he'll be fine," Sir Otto said mockingly. "None of you mummies has any internal organs, as you've just made a big deal of pointing out to everyone."

"You beast!" roared Cleo as her tears mixed with the pounding rain.

The landlord smirked. "Better a beast than a freak like you!" He took Heru's heart from Dixon. "Sorry to stab and go," he quipped, "but now that I've got my first relic, there's work to be done."

Luke and Resus could only watch as Sir Otto led Dixon across the square toward the gates of Sneer Hall.

"Mr. Farr?" said Luke.

"I will survive this," replied the mummy. "You must stop Sir Otto before the spiders smother the life out of Scream Street."

Luke pulled *Skipstone's Tales of Scream Street* from his backpack and handed both to Cleo. "Look after these for me." Taking one final glance at the mummy's tears, he closed his eyes. His friends had been hurt, and that made him angry. It was time to transform.

Sir Otto and Dixon had just reached the gates of Sneer Hall when they heard the growl from behind. Rain battered their faces as they turned to see Luke—now a fully formed were-wolf—prowling across the square toward them.

"You don't want to do this," roared the land-lord, brandishing his sword. "I've got a weapon."

Resus appeared behind Luke, pulling a similar sword from the folds of his cape. "That makes two of us," he snarled.

Thunder crashed as Sir Otto slid the mummy's heart into his jacket pocket and lunged at the vampire. Swords clashed in the rain, flashing brightly as a bolt of lightning illuminated the sky.

"Dixon!" bellowed Sir Otto over the sound of metal against metal. "Get rid of that annoying werewolf once and for all!"

The younger man nodded, his lank hair plastered to his face by the rain. Closing his eyes, he allowed his skin to ripple and stretch as he changed shape once again. Within seconds a large, ginger-haired werewolf stood before Luke.

Cleo clutched *Skipstone's Tales of Scream Street* to her chest. "Luke's dream," she gasped. "It's coming true!"

Chapter Ten
The Fight

Thunder crashed as the two werewolves circled each other, fur flattened against their rippling muscles by the torrential rain. The smaller of the two creatures bared its fangs and howled, the sound echoing around the square.

Dixon lunged at Luke, ready to bite, but the small wolf was too fast to be beaten by such an obvious attack. It flung itself to the ground, back legs pulled up to protect its belly, and lashed out with razor-sharp talons, catching the aggressor's chest and drawing blood. The creature's thick fur was briefly stained red before the rain washed it clean again.

Luke growled as his larger rival appeared in front of him once more, and he braced himself for the attack. It didn't come.

"What are you waiting for?" roared Sir Otto. "Tear out his throat so we can claim the other relics and get in from this cursed weather!"

There was a rippling sound, barely audible over the constant hammering of thunder, and Dixon reappeared. Rain cascaded down his greasy hair.

"Tear out his throat?" he asked, keeping one eye on the snarling wolf before him. "But won't that kill him, Uncle Otto?"

"*Sir* Otto!" bellowed the landlord, swinging his sword angrily at Resus.

"Sorry, Sir Uncle Otto!"

"And yes," his uncle shouted, "tearing the werewolf's throat out *will* kill it. That's the idea." He thrust his sword at Resus. "What's the point of having a shapeshifter in the family if he won't obey your every command?"

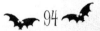

"Maybe he realizes that what you're asking him to do is evil," suggested Resus, knocking the sharp tip of Sir Otto's sword safely to one side.

The landlord's eyes gleamed as another bolt of lightning crackled over the street. "You want evil?" he demanded. "Once I get my hands on *Skipstone's Tales of Scream Street* and the other relics, I'll show you evil!"

Cleo clutched the silver book to her sodden chest. "You'll have to come through all three of us to get this!" she shouted.

Sir Otto grinned. "Now you're just trying to cheer me up," he said. "Change of plan, Dixon. Kill them *all*!"

"All right, Sir Uncle Otto!" Once again, Dixon's skin began to stretch and reshape itself. Within seconds the wolf was back, howling at the sky.

Luke snarled. There was no way he was going to let this monster get to his friends. Dixon leaped across the square; Luke left the ground a split second later. The two wolves met in midair, snapping at each other with yellowed fangs.

The sound of clashing metal caught Cleo's attention, and she spun to see Resus backing across

the square. The vampire stumbled and fell, twisting away as the landlord's sword clanged into the concrete where his head had just been.

Kicking out with a heavy boot, Sir Otto knocked the sword from Resus's hand. It skittered away across the wet pavement, leaving the vampire helpless.

"This is too easy!" yelled Sir Otto, raising his sword high into the air, rain running down the blade and over his hands.

Suddenly a bolt of lightning hit the very tip of his sword, racing down the metal in three raging arcs that burned into the landlord's flesh.

Sir Otto screamed as the force of the blast

threw him back across the square. He smashed into a fence and collapsed, unconscious, blue sparks continuing to fizz along the blade of his sword.

The larger werewolf heard the scream and pulled free of his opponent, swiftly changing back into his natural form as he ran to his uncle's side. Luke was upon him before he had even gotten halfway there, pulling the terrified man to the ground and flipping him over with power-ful paws. The small wolf roared and darted for Dixon's exposed throat.

"Luke, no!" shouted a familiar voice, causing the werewolf's head to snap up. Luke's parents stood across the square, soaked by the storm. Cleo and Resus ran over to them.

"Are you OK?" asked the vampire.

"I wanted to find Luke, to check if he was OK after he saved me," explained Mrs. Watson, unable to tear her eyes away from the werewolf, "but I didn't think he would be . . . I didn't know he had transformed fully."

"He's only changed on the outside," said Cleo. "Luke's still in there."

Mrs. Watson cautiously approached the wolf,

which still sat on the trembling figure of Dixon. "Susan, be careful!" warned Mr. Watson, rooted to the spot on the pavement beside Resus and Cleo.

Luke growled as his mom gazed into his eyes. "You don't have to hurt him," she said softly. "You're better than this. Better than *them*." The werewolf briefly exposed its teeth before whimpering softly and stepping off its victim to lie at its mother's feet.

"Hee, hee!" teased Dixon as he jumped up, unharmed. "The monster wants its mommy!"

Mrs. Watson glared at him and clenched her fists. "Luke is not a monster!" she asserted, swinging an arm around to punch Dixon in the jaw, sending him tumbling over a hedge. "He's my son!"

Resus stood in Cleo's front yard, flaming torch in hand to keep any curious spiders at bay. "Luke's parents are safely home," he said as the front door opened and the mummy joined him. "How's your dad?"

"He's resting," said Cleo. "I think losing my mom for the second time hurt him worse than the sword to the stomach."

Luke appeared beside them, back in human

form once more. "What have I missed?"

"They're back out in force now that the rain has stopped," said Resus. Luke peered along the street. Millions of spiders scuttled over every surface, wrapping trees, fences, and even entire houses in the sticky gray gossamer webbing.

"What do we do?" asked Cleo.

"Short of burning Scream Street to the ground, I have no idea," said Luke.

"You had the spiders under control with the drumbeat for a while," said Resus. "We could try charming them again."

"We lost the only instruments we had fighting Sir Otto and Dixon," said Luke. "We don't have anything that will make a loud enough noise."

Resus suddenly grinned. "Maybe we do. . . ."

"Mr. Howl," called Luke, "we want to hear some more Buddy Bones!"

"At full volume," added Cleo.

Resus pulled a skateboard from his cloak. "If we can drag the jukebox behind us on this," he said, "the spiders might just enjoy the beat of the world's greatest skeleton jazz drummer and come for a stroll!"

The phantom materialized in the yard. "Always glad to get requests from music fans, but two of those Mover guys just carted my jukebox off to Sneer Hall."

"That must have been what Sneer was talking about," said Luke. "He said he was going to surround his mansion with rhythm."

"Why?" asked Resus. "Won't that just *attract* the spiders?"

"Some," said Luke, "but they'll be too affected by the music to spin their webs."

"His house will be safe, while the rest of Scream Street disappears," said Cleo angrily.

"There's nothing we can do, is there?" said Resus.

Luke shrugged. "Not unless we—"

He was interrupted by a sound. A regular tapping that rang out across Scream Street.

Tap, tap, tappity-tappity-tap.

Instantly the clicking and weaving of millions of spiders ceased as the beat floated between the houses.

"Where's it coming from?" asked Cleo.

"Look!" said Resus.

Heru the mummy was tap-dancing on the roof

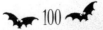

100

of 5 Scream Street. A hatch leading back into the
attic of the Movers' house was open behind him.

Tap, tap, tappity-tappity-tap.

"Didn't you shut him back in his sarcophagus?" said Resus.

"Yes," said Cleo, "but I *may* have left one of
his bandages sticking out, so the lid may not have
locked properly. . . . He is a pharaoh, after all!"

101

"He's not a bad dancer, either," said Luke.

Tap, tap, tappity-tappity-tap.

"But how come it's so loud?" said Resus. "His tapping is echoing right across Scream Street!"

"He's matched the frequency of the spider-webs," said Simon Howl. "He's using the webbing as a giant amplifier! Genius."

"Well, he did say he should have been a star," said Cleo with a grin. "Maybe he should have gotten that soap-opera audition after all."

Tap, tap, tappity-tappity-tap.

Millions of spiders swarmed along Scream Street and up onto the rooftop alongside the tap-dancing mummy. They sat silently, patiently waiting their turn to scuttle back into the attic.

The mummy grinned down at where Luke, Resus, and Cleo stood. "I watched as you tried to save the people of Scream Street from the spiders," he shouted, still tapping. "And I saw you spare the red-haired man's life."

Tap, tap, tappity-tappity-tap.

"Go, Luke Watson," Heru called, his voice vibrating down through the gossamer threads as he danced. "Go and rescue my heart!"

Chapter Eleven
The Light

"**I am NOT happy** about being used as bait," insisted Cleo as Luke and Resus pressed her into a giant spiderweb spun between two trees in the grounds of Sneer Hall.

"You'll be perfectly safe," Resus assured her. "We'll only be behind those bushes over there.

And these spiders aren't going to do anyone any harm," he added. A hundred or so spiders, the only ones now left in Scream Street, crowded around the base of Simon Howl's jukebox as Buddy Bones beat his drums. "I guess the juke-box drowned out Heru's tapping and they didn't follow the others into the attic."

"Right," said Luke, pulling *Skipstone's Tales of Scream Street* from his backpack. "You hold this and act as though you've been caught in the web. When Sir Otto comes to take the book from you, we leap out and get the heart back."

Cleo squeezed his hand.

"What was that for?" Luke asked.

"To say thank you for trying to warn me about my mom." Cleo smiled.

Luke blushed as he and Resus ducked behind a clump of thick bushes. "OK," he called out. "Scream!"

"This has got to be the worst music I have ever heard," roared Sir Otto Sneer as he stomped around the corner of Sneer Hall. He stopped when he saw that the screams weren't coming from the jukebox.

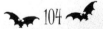

"Well, well," the landlord said with a snort. "What do we have here?"

"Stay back!" yelled Cleo. "I haven't forgotten what you did to my family!"

Sir Otto puffed on his cigar. "Where are your two friends?"

"I'm alone," said Cleo defiantly. "I came to get the mummy's heart for myself."

Sir Otto blew out a swirling cloud of smoke. "If you're here by yourself, why have you got *that*?" The landlord's eyes fell on the silver book in Cleo's hand.

"I stole it," snarled the mummy. "Luke's not the only one with wishes, you know. Now, hand over the heart before I do something you might regret. . . ."

Sir Otto laughed. "My dear little freak! You appear to have misread the situation. Here you are, trapped in a spiderweb, and here *I* am, taking *Skipstone's Tales of Scream Street* for myself. I win again!"

As Sir Otto plucked the book from Cleo's hand, the point of a sword pressed into the scarf around his throat. "You've got it all wrong," said Luke.

The landlord bit down hard on his cigar but remained calm. "No," he snarled. "*You're* the one who's got it wrong!"

A strangled yelp from behind made Luke look around. Dixon stood beside the jukebox, hands around Resus's neck.

"You think I didn't know this was a trap?" said Sir Otto, snatching the sword from Luke. "Dixon, make sure no one finds their bodies."

"What?" shouted Dixon over the drumbeat from the jukebox.

"I said, hide the freaks' bodies once you have dealt with them!"

"I can't hear you," yelled Dixon over a wild cymbal solo.

"You moron!" bellowed Sir Otto. "All I want you to do is—"

Suddenly there was silence. Everyone turned to see Dixon, one hand on Resus's throat, the other pressed against the OFF switch of the jukebox.

"Did you say something?" he asked.

"What have you done?" hissed Sir Otto.

The spiders, suddenly free of the entrancing music, attacked. Luke brushed wildly at them as they swarmed up his legs. Dixon tried to run, but he was brought crashing to the ground by the teeming creatures. Within minutes, Luke, Resus, Sir Otto, and Dixon were all trapped alongside Cleo.

Once the spiders had secured their prisoners, they turned their attentions to Sneer Hall itself, dragging lengths of glistening gossamer up the walls and over the roof. "My beautiful house!" cried the landlord.

"Never mind the house," snapped Luke. "Get us out of here!"

"And how do you propose I do that?"

"Use your cigar!" said Luke.

Sir Otto dipped his head so that the glowing end of his cigar reached the web around his chest. The silky threads shriveled away, and before long he was able to tear himself free. Then he turned to Dixon and released him too.

"Now free us," said Luke.

The landlord waddled over to him, puffing at his cigar. "Do you really think I would help you freaks?" he growled.

"You *have* to let us out!" shouted Luke.

"I don't *have* to do anything," Sir Otto said, grinning. "In fact, from where I'm standing, every-

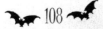

thing seems to be going my way. I have the heart and I have the book."

"By the vampire lords, I will make you pay for this," yelled Resus.

Sir Otto snatched up the silver sword. "I'm sick of you and your freaky friends," he said, and plunged it into the webbing around the vampire's stomach.

"No!" Cleo screamed in terror as the blade sank deep into the gossamer cocoon. Resus doubled over to the sound of breaking glass.

 109

"I'm OK," he breathed. "The sword hit something in my cape."

Sir Otto watched as broken pieces of the spider snow globe fell to the ground. "I won't miss this time," he said, taking aim once more.

"That's Scream Street!" exclaimed Dixon, pointing at the smashed ornament. "There's the central square, and the legs are the side roads."

Sir Otto paused to prod the broken globe with the tip of his sword, dislodging a piece of glass that glistened brightly. Instantly a shaft of piercing light shot up from the model of Scream Street into the landlord's eyes.

"What's going on?" demanded Cleo as Sir Otto fell to the ground, his hand clamped over his face. The light continued to stream from the damaged globe, shooting into the sky and spreading like a blanket over Scream Street.

"It's the sunlight!" said Luke. "Mr. Skipstone said the light was trapped. It must have been in the snow globe, and breaking the glass has released it!"

The webbing around the trio began to melt as it was warmed by the sun. Luke, Resus, and Cleo fell to the ground as their bonds faded away.

"Look!" said Resus, pointing as the thick gray webbing that coated Scream Street's houses and trees began to shrivel up.

Luke grabbed the sword as Sir Otto clambered slowly to his feet, blinking to try to restore his eyesight. He pointed the sword at the landlord's chest. "Cleo," he said, "I think Sir Otto has something for us."

Cleo reached into the landlord's jacket pocket to retrieve the mummy's heart and *Skipstone's Tales of Scream Street*. The author blinked in the bright sunlight. "I can't leave you three alone for a minute, can I?" He grinned.

"You won't get away with this," barked Sir Otto as his vision returned. "Dixon, change into something that can *really* hurt them." The landlord's nephew didn't reply. "Dixon!"

There was a soft whimpering. Dixon was staring up at the walls of Sneer Hall as the patter of tiny feet and the clicking of jaws rang out. The black spiders were returning. "They're coming," he squeaked. "What do we do now, Sir Uncle Otto?"

"*We* won't have to do anything," Sir Otto declared, gesturing toward the jukebox. "Once this is switched back on, those things will leave us alone."

As the landlord reached for the ON button, dozens of smaller silver spiders scuttled over the back of the jukebox, covering the switches. "It's the cleaning spiders!" said Cleo in surprise.

"I guess they do like finding trash after all," Resus replied.

"Dixon," bellowed Sir Otto. "Get rid of them!"

Dixon reached a trembling hand out toward the jukebox, quickly pulling it back as the cleaning spiders clicked at him. "I can't," he wailed. "I'm scared!"

"Here's something to cheer you up," said Resus as he reached inside his cloak and produced a toy monkey identical to the one he had left at the Movers' house. "I told you I had another one of these."

"What are you going to do with that?" sneered Sir Otto as the army of spiders appeared at the edge of the roof and began to scuttle down the walls.

Resus turned the key on the monkey's back a few times, then dipped the toy in the sticky

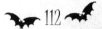

remains of the spiders' webbing. "I'm going to wind you up!"

Luke kept Sir Otto at sword point while Resus stepped behind the landlord and pressed the monkey onto the back of his neck. It began to clash its tiny cymbals together, causing the black spiders to race down the walls of Sneer Hall and crowd around Sir Otto's feet.

"You idiots," the landlord said nastily. "That ridiculous toy will just keep the spiders under my control! They won't harm me."

"That's true," said Luke. "Until it runs down and stops, of course. . . ."

Sir Otto's eyes widened in terror. "Dixon!" he screamed, trying to reach the monkey on his back. "Get this thing off me!"

"I can't reach," whined his nephew, terrified to go too near the swaying black spiders.

Sir Otto turned and ran out into Scream Street, flapping his arms wildly to try to dislodge the toy. The spiders raced after him, clicking happily. Dixon followed at a safe distance.

"I think these are yours," said Cleo, handing *Skipstone's Tales of Scream Street* and the mummy's relic to Luke.

Resus produced a pair of sunglasses from his cape and slipped them on, smiling up at the bright sun that now hung over Scream Street for the first time in decades. "Think we should tease Sir Otto some more?" he asked.

"Nah," said Luke, tucking the book and relic into his backpack. "I don't have the heart for it!"

Tommy Donbavand was born and raised in Liverpool, England, and has held a variety of jobs, including clown, actor, theater producer, children's entertainer, drama teacher, storyteller, and writer. His nonfiction books for children and their parents, *Boredom Busters* and *Quick Fixes for Bored Kids,* have helped him to become a regular guest on radio stations around the U.K. He also writes for a number of magazines, including *Creative Steps* and Scholastic's *Junior Education.*

Tommy sees the Scream Street series as what might have resulted had Stephen King been the author of *Scooby-Doo.* "Writing the Scream Street books is fangtastic fun," he says. "I just have to be careful not to scare myself too much!" Tommy lives in England with his family and sees sleep as a waste of good writing time.